white water

P · J · PETERSEN

SIMON & SCHUSTER

BOOKS FOR YOUNG READERS

SIMON & SCHUSTER BOOKS FOR YOUNG READERS

AN IMPRINT OF SIMON & SCHUSTER CHILDREN'S PUBLISHING DIVISION

1230 AVENUE OF THE AMERICAS, NEW YORK, NEW YORK 10020

COPYRIGHT © 1997 BY P. J. PETERSEN

ALL RIGHTS RESERVED INCLUDING THE RIGHT OF REPRODUCTION

IN WHOLE OR IN PART IN ANY FORM.

SIMON & SCHUSTER BOOKS FOR YOUNG READERS

IS A TRADEMARK OF SIMON & SCHUSTER.

BOOK DESIGN BY HEATHER WOOD

THE TEXT FOR THIS BOOK IS SET IN CANDIDA

PRINTED AND BOUND IN THE UNITED STATES OF AMERICA

FIRST EDITION

1 3 5 7 9 10 8 6 4 2

LIBRARY OF CONGRESS CATALOGING-IN-PUBLICATION DATA

PETERSEN, P. J.

WHITE WATER / P. J. PETERSEN. — 1ST ED.

P.   CM.

SUMMARY: GREG CONFRONTS HIS OWN FEARS AND ASSUMES

A LEADERSHIP ROLE WHEN HIS FATHER IS BITTEN BY A RATTLESNAKE

DURING A WHITE-WATER RAFTING TRIP.

ISBN 0-689-80664-7 (HARDCOVER)

[1. FEAR—FICTION. 2. RAFTING (SPORTS)—FICTION.] I. TITLE.

PZ7.P44197WH   1997   [FIC]—DC20   96-10573

FOR JOE AND CAROLYN BRAUN,
WHO TOOK ME ON
MY FIRST RAFT TRIP

CHAPTER ONE

"I'm *not* going white-water rafting," I said.

"It's my month to choose," Dad said. "And I choose rafting."

"But that's not fair."

Dad just smiled. He had me, and we both knew it.

Dad and Mom were divorced when I was a baby. He had married again and now lived two hundred miles away in a dumpy town called Redding.

On the third Saturday of every month, he came to San Francisco to see me. When I was little, he took me to the zoo or to Golden Gate Park, and I got cotton candy and milk shakes.

But when I got older, things weren't so easy. Dad and I didn't have much to say to each other. He couldn't stand the quiet times, though, so he'd ask me all kinds of lame questions just to keep us talking. And he always wanted to be doing something—like throwing a football or a Frisbee. But pretty soon we'd end up sitting around, saying, "I don't know. What do *you* want to do?"

Sometimes Dad would bring along my half brother, James, who is three years younger than me. James would do the talking for all three of us. And we'd end up doing whatever James wanted.

Finally Dad and I made a deal to take turns planning out our day. On my turn, I could pick anything I wanted. Once we even went to a rock concert at the Oakland Coliseum.

On Dad's turns James usually came along. We had hiked on Mount Tamalpais and Angel Island. We'd been whale watching and mountain biking. But white-water rafting was too much.

"Let's do something else," I said.

"I've been rafting a lot this spring," Dad said. "I even bought a raft last week. I want you to try it. You can fly up to Redding on Friday night and fly back Sunday."

We were sitting in Dad's van in front of our building. We had been to a computer fair and a *Star Trek* movie and a pizza place that had a whole room full of video games. That was the right way to spend a Saturday.

"I don't know if I can go for a whole weekend," I said.

"Let's talk to your mom," Dad said. He put his hand on my shoulder. "There's nothing to be scared of."

I hated it when people said that. Because it was a lie. There was always something to be scared of. I lived in San Francisco, remember? In 1989, I was playing on the sidewalk when the big earthquake hit. It knocked me down, and I had to lie there and watch windows break and bricks come flying. How can you *not* be scared when you know that everything around you could fall down anytime?

Don't get the wrong idea. I didn't sit around all day with my teeth chattering. I just knew that I was never safe, that something bad could happen any minute. So I kept my eyes open. And I didn't take stupid chances.

And that's all rafting was—taking stupid chances. People got into dumb boats with no motors and went down wild rivers just for excitement.

Not me. I already had more excitement than I needed. I was on a bus that was held up by two guys in Halloween masks. And a kid had been shot right in front of my school. And everybody said we were over-due for another earthquake.

Dad and I climbed out of the van and walked up the cement steps to the front door. "It costs too much for me to fly up to Redding," I said.

"That's right," Dad said. "But it's my money."

Before I opened the front door, I checked the sidewalk in both directions. That was a habit. When I pushed the door open, I looked down the hallway to be sure it was empty. Then I stepped inside.

I knocked on our apartment door with my special knock, then used my key to open the door. "Mom," I called out. "Dad's here."

It was hard to believe Mom and Dad had ever been married. When they saw each other, they always seemed nervous. After they said hello and Mom asked about our day, Dad said, "I'd like to have Greg fly up to Redding next month. Could you take him to the airport?"

"Sure." Mom looked at me. "You have big plans for the weekend?"

"Dad wants to go white-water rafting." When a funny look flashed across Mom's face, I saw my chance. "But I don't. Do I have to go?"

I knew it was rotten to try to get Mom on my side, but I also knew it was my only chance.

"Wait a minute," Dad began. "That's—"

Mom held up her hand. "Why don't you go into your room?" she said to me. "I want to talk to your father."

"He can stay—" Dad started. But I got out of there.

Of course, as soon as I got to my bedroom, I stood just inside the door and tried to hear. Mom knew me too well, though. She and Dad went out of the apartment into the hallway.

That was even better. I hurried back to the front door and listened.

"He's a good kid," Dad was saying. "But he's a marshmallow. The minute he breaks into a sweat, he's ready to quit."

"Not everybody wants to be a rough-tough jock," Mom said. Right then, I thought I had a chance.

"I'm not talking about sports," Dad said. "I'm talking about plain old living. He could do all kinds of things, but he won't make the effort."

"I hate to see you pushing him all the time," Mom said.

"Listen, he pushes me too. You think I'd go to rock concerts and horror movies on my own?"

I started to laugh, but I caught myself before I made too much noise.

"If he really doesn't want to go, I hate to have us make him."

"He's got to try new things."

Mom sighed, and I figured she was giving up. "But why rafting?"

"Because that's what I'm doing right now. I want

Greg to try it once. We'll camp out one night and do some fishing. It'll be a nice weekend. If he doesn't like it, he'll never have to go again."

"Watch out," Mom said. "He may come up with a real killer the next month to pay you back."

"It can't be worse than the rock concert. I never felt so old in my life."

"Well, you know how things are these days," Mom said. Her voice sounded different, and I should have known something was wrong. Suddenly the key turned in the lock, and she threw the door open. I had to jump back to keep from being hit.

Mom and Dad looked at me and laughed.

"I was just—" I started.

Dad pointed a finger at me and smiled. "Greg, when you're caught with your hand in the cookie jar, don't start making excuses. Don't say anything at all, except maybe 'I'm sorry.'"

"I'm sorry," I said quickly. And I was. I knew that now there was no way to get out of the raft trip.

But two weeks later I thought I was saved. The fruit fly experiment I did for my science class was selected as one of our school's entries in the city science fair. And the fair was on the Saturday of our raft trip. Right away I called Dad and told him.

After he said "way to go" and things like that, I said, "I guess we can't go rafting."

"No problem," he said. "You can fly up Saturday night after the fair, and we'll go rafting Sunday and Monday."

"I can't miss school."

"Sure you can," Dad said. "I'll call your principal."

Not even fruit flies could save me.

CHAPTER TWO

So on a Sunday morning I ended up riding down a rotten dirt road in a pink bus called The Squealing Pig. My stomach hurt, and I was afraid that the Egg McMuffin I'd eaten in the town of Weed was going to end up on the floor of the bus.

The Squealing Pig was the third sickening ride I'd had in the last twelve hours. The night before, after my fruit flies hadn't won anything at the science fair, I'd taken a nineteen-passenger airplane through what felt like a tornado. Then at five o'clock that morning we'd gotten into Dad's van and broken a few speed records on twisty mountain roads.

Now we were on The Squealing Pig, which wasn't going to break any records, except maybe for noise and dust.

I leaned against the dirty window. I couldn't open it because of the cold and the dust, but I was staying close to it just in case.

Across the aisle from me, right behind the driver, were Dad and James. James was excited about the trip. He'd been rattling on all morning. Finally Dad sent him over to see me.

He came across the aisle and bounced up and down on my seat. "Isn't this neat, half brother?" He always called me that. And he made it sound like something crummy.

"Quit bouncing," I said. "I don't feel good."

"No wonder you're sick," he said. "You ate eggs for breakfast. Eggs make me sick every time."

"It wasn't the eggs. It's this stupid bus ride."

"I think it's neat," James said. "At home the only time I get to ride a bus is for a field trip." He looked over at Dad, then said in a quieter voice, "We get to ditch school on Monday. Isn't that neat?"

"I think I'd rather go," I said.

"Not me. Tomorrow morning I'll be swimming and fishing while Tommy Costa and Eddie Ruiz are sitting in old Room Nine doing math problems. I can't wait."

"I don't think you'll do much swimming," I said. "Dad says the water's still pretty cold."

"We can swim anyway. Unless you're chicken, half brother." James looked at me and laughed. "I'm a good swimmer now. I've been taking lessons all winter in the country club pool."

I knew what he was thinking. He wanted to have a swimming race. He loved to get me into games or contests. Because I was bigger, I was supposed to win every time. And I usually did. But if he beat me or even came close, then it was a big joke on me.

James moved back across the aisle and grabbed Dad's arm. "What kind of bait are we gonna use?"

Fishing. That was one more game where he could try to beat me.

The pink bus belonged to Wild Country Rafting, and all the people on the bus, except us, were either customers or guides. The customers were mostly married couples and college guys. They looked all right, but they had to be morons. Who else would pay eighty dollars to ride on a pink bus and a stupid raft?

Earlier in the spring Dad had been a steady customer. Now he had his own raft and was just hitching a ride with them. I don't know what he paid for the bus ride, but it was too much.

Lucky, the bus driver, was wearing a Harley-Davidson tank top and cutoff jeans while the rest of us were shivering in our sweatshirts. He kept telling Dad about all the rafts that had flipped over. That was scary enough, but whenever Lucky got to a good part in the story, he'd turn around and look at Dad. Meanwhile the bus would be heading straight for a tree or a ditch.

I motioned James over to my seat. "I know how that guy got his name," I whispered. "The way he drives, he's lucky to be alive."

James giggled, then bounced over to Dad's seat to tell him what I'd said. Loud enough for Lucky to hear, of course.

"Watch that," Lucky said.

"I didn't say it," James told him. "It was half brother."

"I've got the camera working today," Lucky said. "You want me to get you guys coming down The Chute?"

I knew what he was talking about. Dad had shown me pictures. A whole raft of people screaming while they were in midair. The Chute was the only spot where the road came close to the river. Lucky would park the bus and climb down there to take pictures of the rafters. Then, if the rafters didn't get killed on the trip, they could buy pictures afterward.

"Don't wait for us," Dad said. "We'll be taking our time. I want to give the boys lots of practice before we get into the big water."

Lucky turned and looked at me. "You ever been rafting before?"

"No."

"I have," James said. "Dad and I went on the Sacramento River last week."

That figured. One more chance for James to make me look bad.

Lucky kept looking at me while the bus drifted toward the edge of the road. "First time's the best, kid. You'll learn in a hurry up here. By the time you get back to Walling's Landing, you'll be an old-timer." He turned forward and yanked the wheel.

"I think we'll camp at Barton's Flat tonight," Dad said. "Then we'll come on in tomorrow."

"That's the way to do it," Lucky said. "We used to do all our trips that way. We'd stop and play volleyball and fish and have a barbecue. But these people are always in a hurry. Gotta do the whole run in one day and get back in town in time for a movie that night."

"I'm gonna catch a whole bunch of fish," James said. "But I don't want to eat 'em. Half brother can have my share."

"Thanks a bunch," I said.

"It'll be great camping on the river," Lucky told Dad. "You'll have the place to yourself. And we're not doing a trip tomorrow, so nobody'll be in your way."

"That's what I figured," Dad said.

"Just hang your food high," Lucky said. "There's a bear hanging around the area."

That was all we needed. If we didn't drown in the freezing river, a bear would get us.

CHAPTER THREE

At the drop-off spot, James and I stayed out of the way while Dad and the guides hauled the rafts off the roof of the bus and carried them to the water's edge. The river didn't look scary. It was bluish green and clear and didn't seem to be moving very fast.

One guide gave the group a safety lecture while the other guides loaded equipment onto the rafts. In ten minutes they were on their way. After the last raft shoved off, Lucky helped us carry our raft down to the water. Our raft was smaller than the others, but it looked the same—a big O with a rower's bench in the middle.

While Dad loaded things and tied them down, Lucky turned the bus around. "See you tomorrow," he yelled. "Say hi to the bear for me."

Attached to the raft every foot or two were metal circles called D rings. "They look like capital Ds," James said, like that was a big discovery.

Dad hooked straps to the D rings and tied everything down. "This way," he said, "if you flip, you don't lose anything."

"Except your passengers," I muttered. James giggled.

"You have to decide what to wear," Dad said, pulling off his jeans. "Everything else goes in the river bags, and we won't open them again until lunch."

It didn't take me long to decide. Like the others, I was wearing jeans and a sweatshirt, with my swimsuit underneath, and I was still cold. "I'll be fine," I said.

James pulled off his jeans, but he kept his sweatshirt after he saw Dad keep his. "Can I go barefoot?" he asked.

"Keep your sneakers on," Dad said. He stuffed the jeans into a river bag and buckled it tight. The river bags were made of black rubber. They were supposed to be waterproof. Since our sleeping bags and food were inside, I hoped they were.

When the gear was all loaded, Dad had to give his

safety lecture. He'd already told us everything on the trip up, but he went through it all again.

He showed us the orange safety line, which was wrapped in plastic. You were supposed to put the loop around your wrist, then throw the bundle. Dad made us slip the loop over our wrists and pretend to throw the rope. He said that in emergencies lots of people got excited, forgot about the loop, and threw the whole package of line into the water.

"Here's the most important thing," Dad said. "If you get tossed in the water, flop over on your back, and float feet first. That way you can use your feet to keep you away from the rocks. That's one reason you don't ever want to take off your shoes. If you end up in the water, the main thing is to relax. Don't panic. The life jacket will keep you up. Just work your way to the side and the quiet water."

What bothered me was that he made this sound like something that was actually going to happen.

We put on our life jackets and our gloves. "Do I have to wear these?" James asked. "I'm not a city boy."

"We don't need blisters," Dad said. "Or whining."

We had two bail buckets. One was a plastic bucket with a metal handle. The other was a one-gallon milk jug with the bottom cut off. "Be careful with these," Dad said, "Keep them clipped to the D rings when you're not using them. And be careful when you're bailing. It's really easy to throw them overboard."

"We're never gonna leave," I said. "We'll end up camping right here." James laughed out loud.

I don't think Dad heard me, but he knew I was complaining. "Don't get in a hurry," he said. "The fastest way is to do everything right the first time."

After some more safety checks, we finally pushed the raft into the water. I held the rope, which Dad called the *painter,* while he and James climbed in. Dad sat on the bench in the middle of the raft, work-ing the two big oars. James and I would sit in the front and paddle. The river bags were in the back to keep the weight even.

After James got settled, I handed him the painter and started to climb over the side. On my last step, I sank up to my ankle in mud. So when I climbed in, I brought gooey brown mud with me.

"Well," Dad said, "now you can clean all that up. We don't want that mess in here."

"I didn't do it on purpose," I said.

"Next time you might sit on the edge and rinse off your foot before you climb in."

That was Dad for you. He was right, of course. He was always right. But he could have saved me a lot of trouble if he'd just said that before I messed up.

We floated along for a few minutes while I tried to clean up the mud. Dad rowed slowly, keeping the raft in the current. Then he had us practice paddling. There were three commands: Forward, Back, and Hold—which meant to quit paddling. James and I knew those in ten seconds, but of course Dad had us keep practicing for a long time.

When we got to sit back and rest, I realized how quiet everything was. We were at the bottom of a steep canyon. Both sides of the canyon were covered with oak trees and brush, with some places where big rocks jutted out.

We floated past two deer—a doe and a fawn— standing on the bank, drinking from the stream. They looked up at us but then went back to drinking.

The sun was warm on my back, and I leaned forward and closed my eyes. For the first time that day, I felt good.

James poked me. "You hear that, half brother?"

I sat up and looked around. Then I heard it—a far-off roar. It was sort of like the ocean, except it was a steady sound.

"Get your paddles ready," Dad said.

We were still on a smooth section of the river, but the roar kept getting louder. It sounded like a waterfall. A big waterfall.

Looking ahead, I could see rocks sticking up in the river, and big waves. "It's a rapid!" James yelled. "A big one."

"This is a straight shot," Dad told us. "Look ahead, and you'll see a V in the water. That's what we aim for. All right. Forward. Keep paddling nice and steady all the way through." By then, he had to shout so that we could hear him over the sound of the water.

I looked ahead. I could see the V. And I could see the rocks and wild waves beyond it.

"We're going, we're going, we're going!" James yelled.

I watched the V come closer and closer. I didn't know what to expect. Judging from the sound, it could have been Niagara Falls.

I leaned over the side, dipping my paddle in the water and pulling, dipping and pulling. I wondered how I was supposed to hang on to the raft and paddle at the same time. I tried to brace myself with my feet, but that didn't help much.

Then the nose of the raft cut right over the V. "Here we go!" James yelled. The raft dipped, and we went diving downward. We smacked the water and bounced. A wave of freezing water poured over me. "Wowee!" James yelled.

The raft climbed a wave, then dipped again. On both sides of us were waves higher than the raft. Water splashed over the sides as we rocked and bounced through the churning water. "Wowee, Wowee!" James yelled.

Then the waves got smaller, and the bouncing slowed. Everything was suddenly quieter. I turned and looked back at what we had been through. It looked a lot smaller than I expected.

"That was neat," James said. "Like a bucking bronco."

"You boys stopped paddling right in the middle," Dad said. "You can't do that."

"I forgot," James said.

"Time to bail," Dad said.

I looked down and saw that my feet were sitting in two inches of water. I hadn't even noticed before, but as soon as I saw the water, I realized that my toes were freezing.

I unclipped the white bucket, and James got the cutoff milk jug. I dipped the bucket into the water and was surprised at how heavy it was. I grabbed the bottom of the bucket with my other hand, lifted the bucket over the side, and tried to throw out the water. The bucket went flying out of my hand and plopped down in the river. James laughed out loud.

"Get it with your paddle," Dad shouted. He dug in one oar and turned the raft toward the bucket.

The bucket was floating upside down, half of it below the water. I reached for it with my paddle, leaning out as far as I dared, but I was two feet short.

The bucket, being carried along by the current,

went on one side of a big rock. That passage was too narrow for us, so Dad had to row like crazy to get us around on the other side, and I had to use my paddle to push us away from the rock.

When we got past the rock, I couldn't locate the bucket. "There it is, " Dad said, pointing behind us.

The bucket was floating along by the shoreline.

"How'd it get upstream?" James asked.

"That's an eddy," Dad said, yanking on his oars. "See how the water is moving there by the shore."

"It can't do that," James said. "Water can't go upstream."

Dad rowed like a wild man, hauling the raft toward shore. He didn't stop until the raft scrunched up against the sand. "You know the whirlpools in the bathtub?" he said after taking a long breath. "That's what eddies are like." He looked at me. "All right. Hop out and get the bucket." I jumped out onto the sand. "Take your paddle. You may need it."

I trotted back along the shore. The bucket was riding lower in the water, resting against a black rock about ten feet out. "It's too far out," I said. "I can't reach it."

"Go in and get it." Dad said. "You threw it in; you pull it out."

The water was even colder than I expected. It was clear up to my knees before I could reach the bucket with my paddle. I worked the bucket close to me, grabbed it, and dumped out the water. When I slopped out onto the bank again, I realized that I should have taken off my jeans.

And, of course, as soon as I got into the raft, Dad said, "Next time you might take off your jeans."

James and I bailed out most of the water. It was impossible to get rid of all of it. It slopped around on the bottom, keeping our feet wet.

"That was fun back there," James said. "For a minute I thought we were gonna flip." He looked over at me. "Wouldn't that be neat—if we flipped over and had to swim?"

"If you boys don't paddle when you're supposed to," Dad said, "that just might happen."

"I forgot," James said. "I was riding the bucking bronco.

"It's fun," Dad said. "But this is serious business too. Forgetting things, even little things like holding on to the bucket, can be dangerous."

That was just what I wanted to hear.

CHAPTER FOUR

We drifted along for a half hour or so. We went through some smaller rapids, and James and I managed to keep paddling. With my feet sitting in water and my jeans still soggy, I couldn't get warm.

"We're coming up to The Chute," Dad said. "This is wild, but it's easier than it looks. We'll go zipping down a long run. You won't paddle until we hit the bottom. Then you'll need to dig in to keep us heading straight."

"This is gonna be great," James said. "In the pictures everybody is screaming their heads off."

"I can't wait," I said. I could feel the fear get hard in my stomach.

"I wish we were getting our picture taken," James said. "I'd take it to school and show Tommy Costa. He thinks he's hot because he rode The Edge at Great America."

The worst part was the waiting. I sat and watched the water and pictured myself in The Chute, scream-ing my head off.

We first heard the roar while we were still floating on flat water. Looking ahead, I could see where the water stopped. And beyond that, just the sides of the rocky canyon.

"Keep your paddles handy," Dad said. "As soon as we hit the bottom, you'll have to go to work. But I'd hold on down The Chute."

With the roar getting louder and louder, I didn't have to be told twice. I grabbed a strap with my left hand, twisting it around my wrist. In my right hand, I held the paddle and another loop. Then I used my legs to brace myself.

"Are you scared, half brother?" James yelled.

"No," I lied.

"I am. I'm gonna scream and scream."

He did too. He was yelling before we even got to the V.

When the front of the raft dipped down, I could see

a long narrow channel, like a water slide. The raft kept gaining speed as we went, bouncing off one side, then the other. I kept a stranglehold on the straps and waited for the whole thing to be over. I closed my eyes once, but the roar and the bouncing were even worse then.

When we smacked down into a pool, I let go of the straps and got my paddle in the water. I tried to pull us forward, but the waves spun us sideways. The raft banged against a rock, and water poured in. "Forward!" Dad yelled. "Forward!" I dug my paddle into the bubbling water, hoping I wouldn't fall out of the raft.

I paddled and paddled, but I couldn't tell if we were going anywhere. All around us were big waves that kept us bouncing up and down. Sometimes I'd reach down with my paddle, and there wouldn't be any water there. Then we'd smack down, and water would pour over me.

Then the waves around us shrank, and soon we were on flat water again. James laughed out loud. "Piece of cake," he said.

I unclipped the bucket and started bailing. I didn't look back. I didn't want to see what we'd been through.

"You guys did fine," Dad said. "It was a little tricky there when we got pushed up against the rock, but we made it. That's the biggest danger—getting shoved up against a rock and having the water pour in. That's how people end up wrapping their rafts."

"Wrapping?" James said. "That sounds like a birthday present."

"It's no present, believe me."

Something in his voice struck me. "Have you done it?" I asked. "Have you wrapped a raft?"

Dad smiled. "Just once. The water was really high. But we got it out."

"Where?" James asked. "On this river?"

"I don't want to talk about it," Dad said. "It's bad luck."

"You know what that means," James said to me. "It means we haven't gone past the place yet."

Once we had finished bailing, Dad said, "We have a nice stretch of easy water now. I want you guys to do some rowing."

"Me first," James said. "Can I have the first turn? Please."

That suited me fine. If my turn never came, that was all right too.

Dad moved to the back of the raft, and James climbed on to the rower's bench. "You won't have to do much rowing," Dad told him. "In a current like this, all you do is keep the raft steady."

James pulled on the oars. "Wow, these things aren't as heavy as they look."

I settled back and rested while Dad had James

work on moving the boat sideways. "This is neat," James kept saying, "It's hard, but it's neat." Every once in a while, he'd let out a laugh for no reason.

"Are you getting tired?" Dad asked him after a while.

"I'll never get tired," James said. "Could you get out the camera? I want to get a picture of me rowing. I want to show it to Tommy Costa."

Dad got the camera out of a plastic bag and handed it to me. I leaned as far forward as I could, but I wasn't sure I could get all of James in the picture. "Tell me when you're ready, half brother," he said.

"Say cheese," I said. James gave me a smile that showed every tooth in his head. He had me take three pictures, to make sure we got a good one.

After Dad put away the camera, he said it was my turn to row.

"I'm not tired yet," James said.

"He can go ahead," I said. "I don't care."

"I want you to try it," Dad said.

So James crawled forward, and I moved onto the rower's bench. It took me a little while to get the hang of rowing. On fishing trips with Dad, I had rowed a boat a few times. But this rowing was backwards from that. I was facing forward, so I was pushing on the oars instead of pulling. But once I got used to the movement, it wasn't too hard.

"Don't make it tough on yourself," Dad said. "Let the current do the work for you."

He had me drag an oar to steer the raft sideways. Once I got the idea of that, I could make little adjustments to keep us in the current.

Floating along, I noticed there were thick nylon strings tied to each oar. The other ends of the strings were tied to the boat. "How come they're tied?" I asked.

"Just in case," Dad said. "We wouldn't want to lose an oar."

"Is that a problem?"

"It's just another safety trick," Dad said. "We don't take chances."

All the talk about safety seemed funny to me. If you really wanted to be safe, what were you doing in a stupid raft?

Just when I thought my lesson was over, Dad said, "Now I'll show you how to ferry."

That was harder work. I had to get the raft turned sideways and then row in the old way. Dad had me haul the raft from one side of the river to the other, over and over.

"I want to try that," James said. "I didn't get to do that."

"I takes a lot of strength," Dad said.

"If half brother can do it, so can I."

I was resting for a minute, just letting us drift, when we suddenly started moving upstream. "Wrong way," James yelled.

"How'd I do that?" I asked.

"That's why you want to stay right in the current," Dad said. "You got off to the side into an eddy."

I had to row really hard to get us out of the eddy and back into the current. "That was tough," I said when we were heading downstream again.

"Do things right, and you'll save yourself a lot of work," Dad said.

I had already figured that out.

It was kind of fun paddling. I learned to watch the river up ahead so that I could plan my moves. If I waited until the last minute, I had to work extra hard to get the raft where I wanted.

We were on a nice flat stretch, and I had the oars out of the water. The sun was overhead, and with all of the rowing, I was finally warm. "Are we gonna eat pretty soon?" James asked.

"It's still early," Dad said.

James looked back at him. "Maybe we could have a snack."

"In a few minutes," Dad said. "You'll need to paddle in a second."

Then I heard the roar of water up ahead. "You take over," I said, sliding off the bench.

Dad pulled me back. "You'll do fine. This is a small one."

"I don't think I'd better," I said.

"You'll do fine. Get your oars in the water."

"You take it," I said.

He put his hand on my shoulder and held me down. "Go ahead and row. Just the way you did before."

I put the oars in the water and started to row. Up ahead I could see black water between two boulders.

"Go right between the rocks," Dad shouted in my ear. "It's a clear shot."

The raft started picking up speed. "Dad!" I meant to say more, but that was all I could get out.

"You can do it," he said. "It's too late to change now. Put us right between the rocks. And aim for the V."

At first, the opening between the boulders didn't seem wide enough for us, and I wondered if I'd have to pull in my oars. But when we got close, I saw that there was plenty of space.

I knew what I wanted to do, but I started to forget things. I wanted clean, slow strokes, but I let an oar drag in the water. That pulled us closer to one side. I knew how to correct that, but I stuck in the wrong oar.

"Use the other one," Dad said, two seconds after I'd figured it out.

I had the raft straight as we passed the rocks, but

we were to the left of the V. I tried to ferry us into position, and the raft turned sideways.

"Woweeeee!" James yelled.

The first waves that we hit banged against our left side, and the raft spun around. Water poured in. I shoved my feet against the sides of the raft, trying not to lose my balance. I didn't try to row. It was all I could do to keep hold of the oars.

Once, in the middle of the bouncing, I realized that I was looking back at the boulders. Before I could think of some way to turn us around, a wave hit us, and the boulders disappeared. A few seconds later, the noise died down, and I was looking ahead at smaller waves. I pushed on the oars and kept the nose of the raft pointed downstream.

"That was neat," James yelled, paddling now. "Piece of cake."

"You know what you did wrong, don't you?" Dad asked quietly.

"Yeah," I said, settling down enough to be mad. "I didn't make you do it."

"You did okay," he said. "You tried to make a correction at the last second, and that got you into trouble. It's always good to go over the V, but the most important thing is to keep the raft straight."

"I told you I wasn't ready," I said.

"That's the only way to learn."

"What if we'd—" I began.

"That wasn't a big rapid. We could have gone over sideways or backwards and been all right."

"Can we get a snack now?" James asked.

"First you bail," Dad said.

I moved forward to help James bail. There wasn't as much water as I expected.

As soon as James clipped the milk jug to the D ring, he said, "Okay, let's eat."

"We have to stop in about five minutes," Dad told him. "We have a big rapid up ahead. I want to look it over before we go through."

It seemed like a lot more than five minutes before we stopped. Finally Dad headed the raft toward a sandy shore. I grabbed the painter, jumped out, and pulled the nose out of the water. I could see the beginning of the rapid downstream from us, and I could hear it better than I wanted to.

"Time to eat," James hollered, taking off his life jacket. "I'll have a cheeseburger and double fries."

Dad took off his gloves and opened a river bag. "How about an apple and some glop?"

"Not as good as a cheeseburger," James said. "But it'll do."

Dad tossed us each an apple, then climbed out of the raft and handed James the plastic sack of glop, which is Dad's own trail mix— oatmeal, raisins, nuts, dried fruit.

Dad pulled off his life jacket and set it in the raft. Then he grabbed a handful of glop and turned away from us. "I'll go look this one over. It changes every day, depending on how high the water is."

"We'll wait right here," I said.

"Yeah," James said. "We'll make sure the bears don't get our glop."

James and I sat down on top of our life jackets. The sun was warm on us, but the sand was still cold. I took some more glop. "One thing about this stuff," I said. "You get so much of it stuck in your teeth, you can snack on it all day."

"Was it fun to row through the rapids?" James asked.

"I wouldn't call it fun."

"I hope I get to do it, I want to see—"

Right then Dad screamed. It was the kind of scream that doesn't leave any question in your mind. James and I jumped up and started running. We knew something was horribly, horribly wrong.

Dad was in the middle of a hillside of boulders, about forty feet above the river. He was staggering around in circles. And he kept screaming.

I went zigzagging through the boulders, leaving James far behind me. My eyes kept bouncing back and forth, flashing up to look at Dad, then back to the ground in front of me.

Dad stumbled against a rock, then slammed into another one. He seemed to have something whitish-brown in his hand that was hanging down toward the ground. I thought it was a stick at first, but it flopped around like a rope. Dad kept jumping around, waving his arm. He was still screaming.

"I'm coming," I called.

Dad threw his hand forward, and the whitish-brown thing smacked against a boulder. "Stay back!" he yelled. "It's a rattlesnake!"

CHAPTER FIVE

I watched Dad raise his arm high, the snake still hanging from his hand. Then he brought down his arm hard, like he was pounding a nail. The snake smacked against a boulder. When Dad held up his hand again, the snake was gone.

Dad came staggering toward me, slamming against boulders that he didn't seem to see. His mouth was open, and moaning sounds were coming out: "Uh-uh-uh-uh." His eyes were huge.

I ran to him. He was holding his bloody left hand out in front of him. The same sounds kept pouring out of his mouth: "Uh-uh-uh-uh." He was breathing with each moan.

I grabbed his right arm, pulled it over my shoulder, and led him downhill. He was hard to steer—heavy and stumbling. The same "Uh-uh-uh" sounds kept coming.

James got behind Dad and held on to his belt. "We got you, Daddy," he said.

Dad's steps weren't straight, but he didn't fall over. I kept pulling him along, heading for the sandbar. It was the only place where he'd be able to lie down.

"Run ahead and get the river bag open," I told James. "Get out a sleeping bag."

James raced to the raft, but he had trouble with the buckle on the river bag. He was still fooling with it when I got Dad to the sandbar. Dad pulled away from me and flopped down next to the water. He lay on his back, then stuck his wounded arm into the river. He let out a yelp when his hand went below the surface.

I grabbed the river bag away from James and got it open. I hauled out a sleeping bag and yanked it out of its stuff sack. "Get the other end of this," I told James.

We laid the bag down beside Dad. He was flat on his back, with his arm in the water. His breathing was a little slower, but he was still moaning with each breath. I unzipped the bag and pushed it up against Dad.

"We want to get this under you," I told him. "Can you lift up a little?"

Dad didn't seem to hear me. Finally I lifted his legs so James could pull the bag under them. After we did that, Dad seemed to get the idea. He raised himself up enough so that we could shove the bag under him. Then he flopped down on the bag, with his eyes closed. James dropped down next to him and put his hand on Dad's shoulder.

I climbed into the raft and opened a metal box in front of the rower's bench. I'd seen Dad put the first aid kit in there. I got the kit, lifted the lid, and started pawing through the packets and bandages.

There had to be something for snakebite. But I couldn't find it. I finally dumped everything in the kit onto the rower's bench and went through it one piece at a time. Nothing.

I climbed out of the raft and knelt down beside Dad. "Dad," I said. "Dad."

His eyes opened, but they didn't seem to see me. "Uh-uh-uh," he moaned.

"Dad, I can't find the snakebite kit."

His eyelids started to close.

I put a hand on the back of his neck and squeezed. "Help me," I said, louder than before. "Where's the snakebite kit?"

Dad's eyes closed. "Don't have one." Those were the

first words he'd spoken since warning me to stay back.

That stopped me cold. I couldn't believe Dad wouldn't have a snakebite kit. Later on, I found out that many outdoors people don't think the kits do any good. But at the time I was amazed. And I felt completely lost.

I squeezed Dad's neck again. "Help me, Dad. I don't know what to do."

He shook his head. "Nothing to do." He opened his mouth again, but it took a long time before anything came out. "Gotta keep it cold. Nothing else to do."

Before I could stand up, James grabbed me and whispered in my ear, "You think he's gonna die?"

"No," I said, trying to sound a lot more sure than I was.

I pulled the raft further out of the water, just to be sure it was safe. Then I plopped down on the sand.

After a while Dad sat up and used his good hand to lift the other one out of the water. He let out a painful holler.

I ran over to him. "Can I help you? Do you need anything?"

Dad shook his head. He started to speak twice before he finally whispered, "Gotta move it in and out of the water. Fifteen or twenty minutes."

James sat beside him, his hand on Dad's shoulder. "I'll watch the time, Daddy," he said.

Dad sat there, his eyes closed, his mouth open and breathing hard. I stood and looked at my watch.

We had just made ten minutes when Dad started to rock back and forth. Pretty soon he was going in slow circles, and I was afraid he was going to fall over. I knelt down beside James, and we helped Dad lie back down. "It's time for the water," I said.

"Only twelve minutes," James whispered.

"Close enough," I said.

Dad eased his arm back into the water, grinding his teeth the whole time. Then he lay back, breathing a little quieter.

Since it was almost noon, I dug into the river bag and got out some of the food snacks. As usual, Dad had brought along plastic tubes of peanut butter and honey. I took a handful of crackers from the box and laid out a row on the side of the raft. Then I squeezed a glob of peanut butter and honey on each one. "You better come eat," I told James.

"I'm not hungry," James said.

I popped a cracker into my mouth. "Better eat anyway."

James got up and walked to the water's edge. He bent down and washed his face. He dried off with the bottom of his sweatshirt.

"His hand looks terrible," James whispered. "Did you see how fat his fingers are?"

"Take some crackers," I told him.

James and I ate a lot of crackers, washing them down with Gatorade. Then we sat and stared at the river. When twenty minutes had passed, we helped Dad sit up and pull his arm out of the river. I kept my eyes away from the hand. "You want some water or Gatorade?" I asked him. He didn't seem to hear me. "You want some water?'

Dad nodded his head. James brought over a water bottle. Dad took it with his good hand, but he was shaking too much. James took the bottle and lifted it to Dad's lips. I guess Dad drank some of the water, but most of it ran down his chin and onto his sweatshirt.

Dad sat there, eyes closed, holding his bad hand against his chest. The fingers were huge, and his whole arm was blowing up. When he started rocking, James and I held on to his shoulders to keep him from falling over. After fifteen minutes we lowered him to the ground, and he got his hand back into the water.

I walked over and sat on the edge of the raft. The time was 12:15. At 12:35, we'd get his arm out of the water again.

I started to think about time. It was Sunday. Nobody expected us until Monday night. After dark on Monday, somebody would figure out that we were having a problem. If they put in a raft at dawn on

Tuesday, they'd probably be here by 7:00 or 7:30.

I counted up. We had forty-three hours to wait. There was plenty of food. I wasn't sure about the water supply, but we could set up the stove and boil some more. James and I could put up a tent. We'd keep Dad as comfortable as we could and keep the arm cold. Maybe I could sleep a little this afternoon so that I could stay awake during the night.

"Uh-uh-uh." Dad was flat on his back with his mouth open. His face was a gray color.

James sat down next to me and grabbed my arm. He leaned close and whispered in my ear, "I'm scared he's gonna die."

"He won't die," I whispered back. "He'll be real sick, but he won't die."

"What're we gonna do?"

"We'll camp here," I said. "Sooner or later somebody'll come along and help us."

"Who?"

"I don't know. Lucky and those guys from the rafting place, I guess. When we don't show up tomorrow night, your mom will get the whole world out to look for us."

James squeezed my arm harder and whispered, "We can't wait that long."

"Maybe I can go get help," I said.

"Where would you go?"

I didn't have an answer for that. I looked across at

the steep canyon walls and knew it was hopeless.

James and I sat for a minute, staring out at the water.

"Uh-uh-oooo," Dad moaned.

"We could go down the river," James said.

"I don't know," I said, but I'd already been thinking the same thing. I was scared of the rapids, but I was more scared of sitting there helpless while Dad got sicker and sicker.

"We could do it," James said.

I reached over for the food bag, rolled down the top, and closed it tight. "It's time to get Dad's hand out of the water," I said.

When we had Dad sitting up, I got right in front of him and grabbed his chin. "Dad," I said. "Dad."

His eyes opened slowly.

"Dad," I said again, "we're gonna get you into the raft. We're going down the river."

Dad shook his head, and his eyelids dropped down. "No," he moaned. "Can't do it."

I squeezed his chin and lifted it. "We've gotta do it. We can't just sit here."

Dad tried to shake his head, but I held it straight. "And you've gotta help. You gotta tell me what to do."

For a minute I saw a light in Dad's eyes.

"We can do it," I shouted. "Come on. We'll help you stand up."

"Yeah," James yelled. "We can do it."

I got on Dad's good side and helped him get to his knees. "Wait," he moaned. He rested for a minute.

"Where's he gonna sit?" James asked.

I hadn't even thought about that. I jumped up and pulled the raft around so that the back end was resting on the sandbar. Then I went back and helped Dad stand up. He kept his arm around my shoulder while he staggered to the raft. I eased him down so that he was sitting on the edge.

I jammed the sleeping bag into its sack, then shoved it into the river bag. Then I grabbed the river bag and tossed it into the raft.

"No," Dad moaned, pointing at the bag with his good hand.

I picked up the river bag, folded down the top, and buckled it tight. It took me a long time because my hands were shaking.

Dad waved me close and whispered. "Front. Tie it."

I wasn't going to argue. I set the bag in the front of the raft. I saw a strap hanging from a D ring, so I just clipped the bag to that strap. It was sloppy work, but I couldn't see any other way to do it.

We got Dad's life jacket on him, then put on our own. I pulled on my gloves. When we were set, Dad leaned back and lifted his feet, one at a time, into the raft. "Wait," he said. He leaned over and put his head between his legs. After a minute he raised his head. "Dizzy," he said.

"You ready to go?" I asked.

He nodded slowly.

I tried to push us loose from the sandbar with my oar, but I couldn't do it. James jumped out of the raft and gave us a push. The raft slid into the water. "Wait for me," he yelled and came diving over the side.

I pushed hard on the oars, pulling us away from shore. Suddenly, for the first time in an hour, I heard the roar of the rapids just ahead.

CHAPTER SIX

"Ferry out to the middle," Dad said. He was leaning forward, but I could hardly hear him. His voice was high and shaky. "Start sideways. Point right. Big rock at the bottom. Stay right."

"Big rock down below," I yelled to James. "We're going on the right side of it."

"Okay," James said. But he didn't sound okay.

By the time I got to the middle of the stream, the current was strong. The raft picked up speed, rocking as it hit little waves. I didn't row much. I just used the oars to keep the nose of the raft pointed to the right.

The water was so choppy, I wasn't sure I saw a V. There was no big drop-off, just huge waves all around us, tossing us back and forth. Whenever we smacked against a wave, water spilled into the raft. There was no way I could steer. I had to pull the oars out of the water so they wouldn't get ripped out of my hand.

Then, straight ahead, I saw a black boulder the size of a car. I shoved my right oar into the water, trying to haul us to the right. The raft spun in that direction, and I lost sight of the boulder. All I could see were waves.

Then we smacked against the boulder. We hit it hard enough so that I got tossed forward, almost out of the seat. I saw James pushing against the rock with his paddle. The raft dipped and turned, and I had my back to the boulder again.

We ended up on the left side of the rock but I didn't care. Just so we were moving. We climbed a huge wave, hung in the air for a second, then shot down the other side. Then we were up in the air again. Some of the time I was jamming an oar in the water, trying to keep us straight. At other times I was just holding on and watching.

Then the rocking slowed down, and the noise dropped off.

"Good job," James yelled. He grabbed the milk jug and started to bail.

I looked back at Dad. He was doubled over, with his head between his knees. "I tried to go on the right," I said.

"Any—" he moaned. "Any, uh, uh, way you can."

The river was quiet for a while. I used the oars to keep us in the middle of the current. Dad had James get a shirt out of the river bag and dip it into the water. Then Dad wrapped the wet shirt around his hand and arm. Looking at the hand made me sick. I didn't see how it could get that big without exploding.

"We're gonna make it," James said, looking back at me. "We're gonna get Dad to the doctor, and everything's gonna be all right."

"You bet," I said.

He held up his paddle. "Look at this," he said. "It looks like a bear chewed the bottom of it."

"You did great," I said.

A scared look came across James's face. "Dad!"

I looked back and saw Dad with his head between his knees again. "Are you okay?" I said. Which had to be about the dumbest thing in the world to say.

Dad didn't answer right away. I looked ahead at the river, making sure nothing was coming up, then turned back to Dad. He was sitting on the back of the raft, the way he had been since we started, but he was leaning way over, with his good hand on the floor of the raft. "Dizzy," he whispered. "Real dizzy."

"You want some water?"

He shook his head, then moved his feet forward and slid down until he was sitting on the floor of the raft. He leaned back and rested his head, his eyes closed. "Uh, uh—that's better."

James looked at me, asking a question without saying a word.

"It's okay," I told him. "He just needs to rest."

We drifted along for a few minutes. James kept turning and looking back, sometimes at me and sometimes past me. He didn't ask any questions. I was glad of that. I didn't have any answers.

When I saw rocks in the river up ahead, I looked over my shoulder. "Dad, what do I do?"

Dad lifted his good hand and brought it straight down. That seemed easy enough.

We went through some choppy water, but I had no trouble keeping us in the middle of the current. James paddled on one side of the raft, then scooted across and paddled on the other side.

A minute later we were on quiet water. Ahead of us was a long stretch of deep blue, smooth river. I pulled the oars out of the water. That way, I could rest my arms. I leaned forward and folded my arms across my chest. I realized that my back and arms were aching. I hadn't noticed before.

I glanced over my shoulder and saw Dad lying

back, his head resting on the top of the raft. His eyes were closed, and his mouth was hanging open. His face had no color at all.

James scooted back toward me and tapped my leg with his fist. "We did good," he said.

"Yeah," I said. "You shoved us away from that rock. I was afraid we were in real trouble there, but you got us off."

"Wait'll I tell Tommy Costa. He's always bragging about stuff he did. I'll bet he's never done anything like this."

"I hope not," I said. "I wouldn't wish this on anybody."

"Tommy Costa's always gotta be the best. You know what I mean? If you say you went to a movie, he says he already saw it. Or he saw one that was better. If somebody hits a big ol' home run, Tommy says he hit one longer than that. He's a big ol'—" He turned away from me and dropped his head.

"You okay?" I said.

He shook his head, keeping his face away from me.

"Listen," I said, "we're gonna make it."

James looked up at me. Tears were running down his face. He reached up and pulled my head down. "I'm scared he's gonna die," he whispered.

"No way," I said. "We're doing fine."

James sat for a minute, then raised up and whispered, "What's it like not to have a father?"

"You're nuts," I whispered. "I have a father."

"You know what I mean," James said.

"I have a father," I said. "And I'm gonna keep having one. We're gonna make it."

James used the sleeve of his sweatshirt to wipe the tears from his face. "Aren't you scared?"

"Yeah, I'm scared. Listen, Superman would be scared if he were here." That made James smile for a second. "But it's okay. We're gonna make it."

"Right," he said.

"But you gotta help," I told him. "You gotta do two guys' jobs up in the front."

"I can do it," he said.

"You better."

He scooted forward. "Don't worry about me."

I could see rocks in the water up ahead. I tapped on Dad's leg. "Dad. Dad." I tapped harder. "Dad!"

His eyes snapped open. "What?"

"We're coming up on some rocks," I said.

He leaned to one side so that he could look around me. I waited for a minute, then looked back at him.

His eyes were almost closed. "Middle," he mumbled.

I don't know if Dad stayed awake through those rapids or not. I had my eyes on the water in front of me. I spotted the V early and went right through it. The raft bucked and jumped in the rough water below, but I kept the nose heading downstream. James paddled the whole time.

Then we had another long stretch of quiet water. Dumb things happened. When we'd started out, I'd been too scared to think about anything but rowing. But you can't stay that scared for long. Floating along on the quiet current, I started thinking about Lucky and the pink bus. And guys in my school. And Mom driving around in her old Toyota. And then I was remembering a time when James was about four years old and he sang "Itsy Bitsy Spider" for me. After that, I couldn't get that stupid song out of my mind.

There I was in the raft, scared to death, knowing how careful we had to be. And I was humming "Itsy Bitsy Spider."

"Here we go," James shouted.

I had been in a fog. Once James yelled, I woke up to the far-off sound of pounding water. I could see a long stretch of flat water ahead of me. If the rapids were that loud already, they had to be big ones.

"Dad," I shouted over my shoulder. "Hey, Dad. What do I do? Dad? Dad!" I turned and looked back. Dad was lying back, his eyes closed. His mouth was hanging open, For a second, I wondered if he was dead. "Dad!"

"He's sleeping," James shouted.

"He's gotta wake up," I said. "Dad! Dad!" I pulled in an oar, then reached back with that hand and grabbed Dad's leg. "Wake up!"

Dad's eyes opened about a quarter of an inch, and his head flopped to one side.

I shook his leg. "Wake up!"

"Greg!" James yelled over the roar of the water. "Get ready!"

The boat was rocking in the choppy water. I gave Dad's leg one more hard yank, but his eyes stayed closed. I grabbed my oar and shoved it into the water. Then I looked ahead into the black water, trying to locate the V.

James and I were on our own.

CHAPTER SEVEN

Ahead of us was a drop-off. I had no idea how big. All I could see was black water, then nothing.

I took a quick glance over my shoulder. Dad's eyes were still closed. I reached back and hit his leg and yelled at him again. But with the crashing of the water, I could hardly hear my own voice.

The raft rocked and tossed while we headed for the drop-off. James was sitting on the left side, holding his paddle a few inches above the water. He looked back at me, smiling, and yelled something I couldn't hear. Maybe "piece of cake."

We were being swept along by the fast-moving current. I kept the nose of the raft straight and searched for the V. When we got close to the edge, I could see the river up ahead. After the first drop, which I still couldn't see, we had about a hundred yards of flat water before we went down a second drop. I took a long breath. Somehow things were better if I could see what was coming.

But first we had the drop. Five feet from the edge, I shoved down on both oars to lift them out of the water. I braced my feet against the sides to hold me on the seat. But when the front of the raft suddenly dipped down, I still slid forward.

After the first short drop, we bounced to the right, then made two more quick drops. When we hit the wild water at the bottom, the raft was almost sideways. I shoved an oar into the water to straighten us out.

Just then the right side of the raft rose high into the air. I felt myself sliding sideways off the seat. Then I saw James go flying into the water, and I knew I was going with him.

I smacked the water headfirst and went plunging down. The cold hit me like a hammer. For a minute the only things I knew were cold and darkness. Water poured into my nose and mouth.

I had to get a breath. My lungs ached, and I was choking. I kicked and tore at the dark water around me. I had no idea where the surface was, but I couldn't stay where I was. I could feel my body moving, carried along by the current. I kicked harder. Then my head popped out of the water. My mouth flew open, and I sucked in air.

A wave hit me in the face and filled my mouth with water. I turned sideways, spit, and sucked in another breath. I didn't know where I was, and right then I didn't care. I just wanted air. Lots of air.

My shoulder smacked a rock, and my elbow banged against it as I was swept past. I tried to swim, throwing my arms ahead of me in a wild dog paddle.

I smacked my hand into another rock. That hurt bad enough to wake me up, and I remembered Dad's lecture. I turned onto my back and got my feet out in front of me. That way, I could protect myself from the rocks. And, I discovered, I could see where I was going.

I still had a stretch of flat water before the next rapids. Off to my right I could see a curve of sandy beach. I paddled in that direction.

I spotted Dad downstream from me, floating in quiet water. But I couldn't see James. Looking around, I saw our raft rocking along in the current. Then, while I was still watching, it suddenly disappeared over the edge. With a sick feeling, I wondered if James had gone the same way.

I stopped paddling and turned back upstream. There was James, about ten feet behind me. He raised his hand and yelled something. I let out the breath I didn't realize I'd been holding.

So we were all right. Alive anyway.

But once I saw that we were safe, my mind flashed back to the raft. All of our food and our camping gear was on that raft. And I had just seen it go flying over the rapids.

For a minute my mind was flooded with questions about what we'd eat and how we'd stay warm. But it was too much at once. I closed my eyes for a second and took a huge breath. When I opened my eyes again, I tried not to think about anything but paddling.

I didn't realize how shallow the water was getting until I banged my heel on the bottom. I stood up and waded out toward James. I grabbed hold of his life jacket and pulled him into shallower water. "You can stand up here," I said.

James put down his feet, stumbled once, then got squared away. "Let's get Dad," he yelled.

"Right," I said and started wading in that direction. James ran toward shore, then raced downstream in the shallow water.

Dad was floating in water too deep for wading. I walked in as far as I could, then leaned forward and started to dog-paddle toward him. James ended up alongside me. Dad sort of smiled when we came close. "We got you, Daddy," James said. He and I grabbed hold of Dad's life jacket and towed him toward shore.

We kept towing him even after the water got shallow enough for us to wade. I didn't think Dad could walk, and I knew we couldn't carry him. When his feet started dragging on the bottom, I reached down and lifted them. We scooted him into ankle-deep water.

Dad used his good hand to push himself into a sitting position. He looked at us and tried to smile. "Bad way to wake up."

"I don't know what happened," I said. "It didn't look that bad. Then all of a sudden we flipped over."

"Gotta get dry," Dad said.

I hadn't been thinking about the cold. Once I did, I realized how much I was shivering.

We helped Dad scoot up onto the sandy shore. Then we spent a long time getting off his life jacket.

The sun was almost directly overhead. It felt good on my wet head.

"You want your sweatshirt off?" I asked.

"Everything," Dad said. His whole body was shaking with the cold.

We got the sweatshirt all the way off except for the

bad arm. I was afraid to try to pull it over that hand. "Leave it," Dad said. We pulled off his swim trunks and his soggy shoes.

Dad curled up in a ball with his back to the sun. He lay there on the sand, shivering. "Get your clothes off," he told us.

James came over to me and whispered, "Did the raft sink?"

"No," I said. "But it went over the rapids down there."

"Oh no," James moaned. He started to ask something, then turned away and pulled off his life jacket and sweatshirt. "You'd better get off your wet stuff," he said.

I sat down on the sand. "I gotta rest a minute first."

That was only partly true. I did need the rest, but I also needed to think. I looked down at my watch. I knew for sure now that it was waterproof. The time was 1:30.

An hour ago we'd had food and sleeping bags— everything we needed. If I'd been smart, at least we'd have been comfortable. But back up there, I'd thought things couldn't get any worse. Wrong again.

The best we could hope for now was to have somebody get here on Tuesday morning. So we had two cold nights ahead of us, and we had no food, no fire— nothing but the wet clothes on our backs.

I had to do something. I couldn't just sit and wait for two days. Maybe I could build some kind of shelter for us. There were some piles of driftwood here and there. Maybe I could use sand to build walls and then make a roof of driftwood.

I looked over at Dad curled up on the sand. His whole body was shaking. He needed a lot more than a sand-and-driftwood shelter.

I stood up quickly. There was only one thing to do. Somewhere downstream was our raft. I had to find it and get our supplies.

I looked in that direction. On our side of the river was a cliff. It was only about thirty feet high, but it might as well have been a thousand. It wasn't straight up and down; it was worse than that. The same water action that had made the sandbar had eaten away at the rock. The bottom of the cliff looked like it had been scooped away with a giant ice-cream scoop. It would be impossible to climb. I'd be bending over backwards.

I looked upstream to see if there was any way to get around the cliff. Nothing but steep rock faces.

On the other side of the river, though, things looked better. There were boulders and some rocky outcroppings. I was pretty sure I could work my way downstream over there.

By then, James had his clothes spread out to dry.

He stood on the sand with his arms held tight against his chest. "I'm freezing," he said.

"You'll warm up pretty soon."

"You'd better get your clothes off too."

"I'm going downstream," I told him. "Maybe I can find our raft. Things will be a lot better tonight if I can get our sleeping bags and some food."

James looked at the cliff. "You think you can climb that?"

"No. I'm going across the river."

"Oh, man, that's worse."

I stepped into the water. "I might as well get going."

"Be careful," James said.

Dad rolled over partway and looked up at me. "Don't—" he said.

"I'm gonna get our stuff," I said. "I'll be back in a little while."

Dad's mouth opened again. I turned toward the water. It didn't matter what he said. I was going after the raft.

Below me, not too far above the second set of rapids, the river seemed wider and shallower. I waded downstream until I found a place where the water didn't look quite so deep. I gave James a wave and started across.

The water swirled around my legs as I walked. I

took my time, making sure my front foot was solid before moving the back one. By the time I was halfway across, the water was up to my waist. I held my life jacket high to keep it out of the water.

I walked bent over, looking through the water at the rocky river bottom. I was trying to spot flat places to put my feet. Every few steps, when both feet were solid, I'd glance up and see how close I was getting to the other shore. I didn't look behind me at all.

I tried not to look downstream. I didn't want to know how close I was to the rapids. The noise of the pounding water was so loud that I couldn't hear anything else. I only noticed that, though, when I banged my ankle against a rock and yelled, "Ow!" I could hardly hear my own voice.

Inching forward through the swift water, I must have seen something out of the corner of my eye. I planted both feet, than looked downstream. My eyes moved past the black water, automatically spotting the V. Most of the rapids were out of my sight, but I could see a long stretch of the river below. The closest water I could see was still choppy, but then the river widened into a patch of greenish blue. And at one edge of that patch was a bright yellow spot—our raft. It was floating upside down, close to the shore.

"All right!" I yelled. I couldn't hear the words, but I didn't care. Everything was possible now. I could hike along the far bank, wade the river again, and get to the raft. Up until then I'd been afraid that the raft would stay in the current and just keep floating. But our luck had finally changed.

I turned and looked back at James. He was sitting in the sand, his legs pulled up against his chest. "I see the raft!" I yelled. He waved, but I didn't know if he actually heard me.

I looked back at the stream in front of me. I still had another twenty feet to go. But I could do it. Right then I felt like I could do anything.

I took a step, got one foot square on the rocks, then lifted the other. When I set down that foot, the water rose on my stomach two or three inches. The current tugged at the bottom of my life jacket.

I braced my feet and lifted the life jacket. I looked ahead at the water, trying to see if it was even deeper. I couldn't tell. But it didn't make much difference. Deeper water or not, I had to get across.

I took another step. My foot landed on a loose rock. I shifted my weight to my back foot and felt the current pull me. I shoved down on my front foot, but it was too late. I stumbled sideways, and the river pulled me off my feet and swept me along. I dragged my feet on the rocky bottom, trying to stop myself. All that did was send me over onto my stomach.

I lifted my feet and leaned backwards, reaching my

arms out wide. In no time at all I was in the old position, floating feet first. The waves rocked me up and down. I looked ahead, between the toes of my tennis shoes, and saw the V.

I was making a perfect approach. Except that I was minus a raft.

CHAPTER EIGHT

I don't think I was scared right at first. I was too surprised. One second I was standing there, waist deep in water; the next, I was zipping downstream.

Once I got onto my back, I took a deep breath. I looked ahead, between my tennis shoes, and saw the V coming at me. I grabbed my life jacket with both hands. I don't know why. But it was something to do.

I shot over the edge and seemed to hang in midair for a minute. I had plenty of time to get a good look at the rocks and the wild water that were waiting for me. *Then* I was scared.

I don't remember screaming, but I must have been doing it. I know because I got a mouth full of water when I hit the first wave.

The wave threw me sideways. My feet banged against a rock, and the current pulled me away. I didn't try to swim. Even if could have done anything in those waves, I wouldn't have known which way to go. I just held on to my life jacket and hoped that the current would take me through.

Then I was underwater. I closed my eyes and held my breath, waiting to pop out again. But that didn't happen.

Thoughts of whirlpools flashed through my mind. Maybe I was being sucked down and down. I started kicking and pulling at the water. I opened my eyes, but I couldn't see anything but bubbles. I kept grabbing at the water, trying to fight my way out.

I couldn't tell if I was making any difference. But I kept fighting the water because I couldn't stand to be still.

Then it was just too much work. My arms and legs were getting too heavy to move. I was finished. And I was almost too tired to care.

I gave one last frog kick, but it didn't seem to help. The bubbles kept swirling in front of my eyes.

When I popped out of the water, I was so surprised, I only got part of a breath before my head went under again. But I bobbed back up and sucked in all the air my lungs could hold.

I immediately flipped onto my back. I could breathe easier that way. So I'd learned something at least.

I didn't try to paddle. I let the current carry me through the swirling waves. I was still unbelievably tired.

Ahead of me, off to the right, was the yellow raft. I shoved my right arm down and used it to steer me that way. The current carried me exactly where I wanted to go. I came floating straight for the raft, watching between my feet as it got bigger and bigger. I felt like a plane coming in for a landing.

Just upstream from the raft, I shoved down my feet and stood up. The water came just below my waist. The river swirled around me, but I could keep my balance.

Standing there, I tried to figure out what had happened. The raft was about fifteen feet from the shore, floating upside down. The current wasn't strong, but there *was* a current. The raft shouldn't have been sitting where it was. It had to be caught on something.

Stepping carefully, I moved up close. On each side of the raft, an oar was floating, held there by the nylon lines. So one of Dad's safety tricks had worked anyway.

Floating next to the oar on the right side of the raft, bobbing up and down, was the painter. That meant the front of the raft was pointing upstream.

I grabbed the painter and headed for shore. When the rope was tight, I gave a yank. The raft barely moved. I pulled again, and it shifted a few inches.

I couldn't see what was holding the raft. I waded upstream and yanked on the rope again. The raft came toward me a little, but not enough.

I moved next to the raft and gave it a hard push. Then I realized how stupid that was. What if I shoved the raft free? I'd be left standing there, watching it float away.

I tied the painter to my belt. I wondered whether the raft, if it suddenly broke free, could yank me off my feet. But I started pushing and shoving just the same.

I could move the downstream part of the raft to one side or the other, but the upstream part wouldn't budge. I waded back there and pushed some more. The raft was hung up close to where the painter was attached. But I couldn't understand how it could be caught there.

I moved next to the raft and reached as far underneath as I could. When I squatted down, the life jacket lifted me up again.

I stood up and stepped back. I hated to do it, but I

had to take off my life jacket. It took me a long time to unsnap the buckles with my cold fingers. I started to put the life jacket on top of the raft, but decided that would be dumb. I waded toward shore. The shoreline was a gravel bar with some big rocks sticking up. It would be an easy place to haul out the raft—if I could get it loose.

Halfway to shore, I was stopped by the painter, which was still tied to my belt. I raised the jacket over my head and threw it onto the gravel.

I waded back to the raft and reached underneath. I kept stretching until my head was jammed against the raft and my chin was touching the water. My fingertips touched something slick. I pushed on it, and it gave a little. It was like pushing a balloon.

Then I knew what it was. The river bag. Being in a hurry, I had clipped it to a strap hanging from a D ring. Now that the raft was upside down, the bag was hanging below. It must be caught on a rock or something.

I took a big breath, then ducked my head underwater. I tried to grab the bag, but it was too big, and there was nothing I could get hold of.

When I tried to stand up, I felt my feet slipping. I dug in my heels, reached back over my head for the outside of the raft, and pulled myself out.

I held on to the raft and got my breath back. My

teeth were chattering, and my hands were shaking. I had to hurry.

The strap had clips on each end. Even with my hands shaking, I could open a clip—if I could get to it.

I was about to go under when I remembered the painter. If I got the raft loose, I wasn't sure I could hold it, especially without my life jacket. I hated to take the time, but I could hear Dad saying, "The fastest way is to do everything right the first time." I spotted a rock sticking out of the water. I waded over and tied the painter to it.

Back at the raft, I took four deep breaths, then ducked my head underwater. I couldn't see much, but I got my left hand on the river bag, I took two short steps to get closer. My leg banged into something solid. I reached down and felt slick wood. Some kind of limb. But it was the top of the bag I was interested in.

I tried to work my hand up between the bag and the raft, but they were pressing against each other. I couldn't squeeze my fingers in between.

Feeling my chest get tight, I ducked down, backed up, and raised my head above water. While I took in some long breaths, I tried to picture what was down below.

The bag was hung up on a limb. That meant the raft was being held there by the bag. No wonder I couldn't get my hand in between. I had the whole weight of the raft pushing against the bag.

I had to go around and reach the upper clip from the front. I didn't like getting that far under the raft, but I had no choice.

I took another breath, ducked down, and got hold of the river bag. I kept my hands on the smooth bag while I moved around it. My knee banged against the limb. I leaned forward, reached out, and ran my left hand up the bag.

Then I had it, the strap that was clipped to the D ring. I shifted my feet and slid my fingers up the strap.

In the same second, I felt three different things: I felt my fingers break the surface of the water, I felt the slick metal of the D ring, and I felt my throat get tight. I had to get air soon.

I probably would have let go and moved backwards if I could have. But I wasn't sure I could make it. And I knew where there was air. My fingers had felt it. I raised up quickly, bumped the raft with the top of my head, then turned my head sideways and felt my face come out of the water.

I let go of the breath I'd been holding and sucked in new air. I couldn't see a thing, but I still had my hand on the D ring. I worked my other hand over there and got my fingers on the clip.

My fingers didn't have much feeling in them, but I

knew what I had to do. My thumb had to push open the clip. Then I had to turn the clip to free it from the D ring.

It took me three breaths to get the clip open. Then it wouldn't turn. I used my other hand to lift up on the strap, fighting for a quarter inch of slack. The clip wiggled in my hand.

Then the raft banged against my head, knocking me to my knees. Suddenly I was in the sunlight. I staggered to my feet and looked around for the raft.

I stood there, holding the river bag by the strap. and watched the raft float downstream. The painter straightened out, then got stiff. I held my breath, but the raft stopped. It sat there, bobbing up and down.

Now that I could see, the river bag was no mystery. It was caught in the fork of an old tree limb. The limb was white, all of its bark gone. I yanked the bag free and carried it to the shore.

Then I went back and tried to untie the painter. My hands were shaking too much, though. I couldn't do anything with the knots. I had to go ashore and get a knife out of the river bag to cut the rope. Then I pulled the raft to shore.

The rower's bench was a few inches higher than the sides of the raft, so it was the first thing that got jammed into the gravel. That left the raft half in the water, without enough space for me to squeeze underneath.

I had to get under there. I tried to lift one side, but the raft scooted backwards. I tried twice more before I stopped and looked around. Just upstream, a few feet from the water's edge, was a good-sized boulder.

I shoved the raft back into the water and pulled it along until I was even with the boulder. Then I hauled the raft out of the water and started working one side up onto the boulder. By getting down low and lifting and pulling, I could scoot it up a few inches at a time. The oar was in my way, but I didn't want to cut the nylon string.

I stopped when I had that side about two feet off the ground. That gave me enough room to crawl underneath and got whatever I wanted.

Before I did anything else, I went to the river bag and pulled out my dry clothes. I even found a towel in there. It took me a long time to strip off my soggy jeans and sweatshirt. Then I used the towel to dry myself off, and pulled on those dry clothes. Nothing in my life has ever felt so good.

My legs and arms ached. I just wanted to lie down. But I had work to do first.

Right there in the open river bag were our sleeping bags. If I got those to Dad and James, they could stay warm. Everything else could wait.

I grabbed a sleeping bag in each hand and headed up the shoreline. In front of me was a gravel bar and then a long rocky hill. There was no cliff on this side, just a steep steady rise. I picked my way between the rocks and climbed to the top. I stood next to a scraggly pine tree and looked down at the sandbar where Dad was lying. James was curled up next to him.

"James!" I yelled. "Hey, James!"

James sat up and looked around.

"Up here! Hey! Up here!"

When James finally spotted me, he came running toward the cliff. "Are you okay?" he shouted.

"I'm fine. I even got dry clothes on."

He looked up at me. "I thought you were dead. I saw you get washed away. I thought you—" He broke into a sob.

"Hey, I'm fine," I said. "Stand back. I'll throw down these sleeping bags."

James moved back a few feet, and I let the bags drop. "This is great," James said, grabbing the bags. "Thank you, thank you."

"Get Dad into one of them," I said. "I'll go back and get you some clothes."

With a bag in each hand, James went running back toward Dad. "Thank you, thank you," he yelled over his shoulder.

CHAPTER NINE

I made two more quick trips up the hill. First, I crawled underneath the tipped-up raft and got the other river bag loose. I dumped everything in the bags onto the gravel and got dry clothes for Dad and James. I wrapped the clothes in a shirt of Dad's, hauled them to the top, and dropped them to James.

"Thank you, thank you," he yelled. By then, Dad was curled up in a sleeping bag.

For the second trip, I used a river bag. I put in the stove and the tent and all the food. I also put in the first-aid kit, although I didn't know if there was anything in it that would help. I carried the bag up the hill and dropped it over the cliff for James.

After that, I wasn't in such a hurry. And I was exhausted. I sat down on the gravel for a minute, then closed my eyes and lay down. I know I went to sleep, because I dreamed about Dad with the snake hanging from his hand. I woke up yelling.

I sat for a minute and let my heart slow down. It scared me that I'd gone to sleep so easily. What if I'd slept a long time? What if I'd slept until dark?

I had work to do. Unless I was going to spend the night where I was, I had to figure some way to get to the bottom of the cliff.

Somewhere in the raft was the safety rope. Dad had made us practice with it, but I wasn't sure where he'd put it afterward. If I got the rope, maybe I could use it to climb down.

I crawled under the raft again. In front of the rower's bench were two metal boxes, but I couldn't see well enough to tell how they were attached. I crawled back out to get a flashlight. But once I was in the sunshine again, I changed my mind. Instead of crawling around in the half-dark, why not just turn the raft over?

I worked the raft higher up onto the rock. I pushed and yanked, shoved and lifted. Pretty soon I had the high side about five feet off the ground. The raft wasn't straight up and down, but it was close. If I'd been eight feet tall, it would have been easy to shove it on over.

I needed a good stick. I thought about cutting the oar loose, but it was too long for what I needed. I jogged across the gravel bar and looked around the rocks, where there were piles of white driftwood. I dug out three or four long sticks, all too big. I kept digging until I found exactly what I wanted—a slick limb a little fatter than a baseball bat. And one end of it was smooth enough so that I wouldn't have to worry about poking a hole in the raft.

I hurried back to the raft, got underneath, and used the limb to push against the top. I raised the raft, a few inches at a time, until I felt it rocking. I shoved up on my limb, and the raft teetered, then came crashing down with a tremendous *whop*.

Most of the raft ended up sitting in the shallow water. I grabbed the painter and hauled the raft up onto the gravel bar. Then I stepped inside and looked around. I found the safety rope right away. It was clipped to a D ring in front of the oarlocks.

Before I unclipped the rope, I opened the metal boxes. One box had emergency supplies—freeze-dried food, two space blankets, water purification tablets, and some bandages. I felt better when I saw those things. If we had to wait two days to be rescued, at least we wouldn't be cold or hungry.

In the other box was another coil of rope, but it was hooked to a set of pulleys. I know now that what I was looking at is called a block and tackle. Raft runners carry them in case they have to free a raft stuck on a rock.

I had played with pulleys in my science class, but right then I couldn't see any use for them. I was only interested in the rope. But since it was skinnier than the safety rope, I left the whole thing in the box.

I gathered up the emergency supplies and the safety rope, stuffing everything into the other river bag. I put my wet clothes on top of the rest, then carried the bag up the hill. From the top of the cliff, I looked down at James. He was sitting on the ground with his face in his hands.

"Hey, James," I called. "I got some more stuff."

When James turned and looked up at me, I could see the tears shining on his cheeks. "Dad's not doing too good," he said. "He's been puking."

I took the safety rope out of the bag and set it aside. "Move back," I told James. I swung the bag back and forth a couple of times, then let it go on the next forward swing. The bag sailed through the air, then dropped down, picking up speed, and hit the ground with a thud. That sound made me nervous. If I slipped off the rope, that's the sound my body would make when it hit.

I tied the safety rope to the trunk of the scraggly pine tree, wishing that I knew a fancy knot. I had to settle for six granny knots. It wasn't pretty, but I figured it would hold me.

Before tossing the rope over the cliff, I stopped and sat down. I was a little nervous, but that was only part of my reason for stopping. Down below me James was kneeling by Dad, taking the things out of the river bag. Dad wasn't moving at all.

I glanced at my watch. It was almost three o'clock. Nobody would be coming for forty hours. Maybe longer.

What was I going to do for forty hours? Sit there with James and watch Dad get sicker and sicker? Would Dad last that long?

"No," I said aloud. I wasn't going to climb down there and sit. I had to try something. Anything.

What if I went down the river alone? If everything went right, I could get to Walling's Landing tonight, and the rescuers could be here tomorrow morning. And they could bring a doctor along.

I stood up and looked over the cliff. I could let down the safety rope, and James could put whatever I needed in a river bag. Then I could haul it up.

What did I need? Some food and water. There was no point in taking my wet clothes.

I wouldn't need my sleeping bag unless—unless—

there was the problem. If I had trouble and flipped the raft, things would be really bad. What if I ended up stuck downstream somewhere? I'd be there without any supplies, and I wouldn't be any help to Dad.

If I was really careful, could I make it downstream? I thought about that for a minute. I'd been careful before, and I'd dumped us in the river. And I'd been careful crossing the river, and had ended up swimming a second time.

Being careful wasn't enough. I had to have help from somebody who knew the river. And the only person like that was lying down below me in a sleeping bag.

For a minute I thought about getting Dad down to the raft. But he couldn't go over that rapid. And I sure couldn't haul the raft upstream.

I even thought about using the pulleys to get Dad up the cliff. In our science class, one little girl, using pulleys, had lifted our fat teacher off the ground. But pulleys were only good for short distances, not thirty feet. You couldn't stop halfway up the cliff and redo your ropes.

I sat down on the ground again. There was no hurry now. I couldn't make the trip downstream by myself, and there was no way to get Dad to the raft. So the only thing left was to wait. And wait.

I was sitting there, staring down at the river, when

the idea hit me: If I couldn't get Dad to the raft, maybe I could get the raft to Dad. It seemed like a crazy idea at first. But there was no reason not to try it. I had nothing else to do.

"I'll be back in a while," I yelled at James.

James got up and ran to the bottom of the cliff. "Aren't you coming down here?"

"In a little while."

"Good. I hate being here by myself."

CHAPTER TEN

I ran down the hill to the raft. Time was a problem now. We had to get onto the river soon if we were going to make Walling's Landing before dark.

While I ran, I looked around for the best path. The first part looked easy. I'd tow the raft as far upstream as I could. That would cut down on the distance I had to cover.

I put the oars in the raft and tied them down. Then I grabbed the painter and shoved the raft back into the water. There was almost no current along the shore, so towing the raft wasn't hard.

But when I dragged it up onto the gravel bar again,

it felt like somebody had dropped rocks in it. I coiled up the painter and set it in the raft. Then I opened the metal box and took out the rope and pulleys.

What I had were two metal bars with wheels on the bottom—sort of like in-line skates. But there was a rope connecting all those wheels. If you pulled on the rope, it ran through all of the wheels and slowly moved the two bars closer together.

I know it's hard to picture this thing, but what all of the wheels do is multiply your force. With the pulleys, you can lift five or six times what you can without them. But it's slow. I had to pull about six feet of rope to move the metal bars one foot closer together.

So what I figured was this. I could hook one bar to a rock and the other one to the raft. Then I could pull on the rope and move the raft up to the rock. Then I'd move the first bar to another rock, pull on the rope, and move the raft again. So up the hill I'd go, a few feet at a time.

I hooked one bar to a D ring on the front of the raft. Then I separated the two bars, watching the rope run over the wheels. I ran out of rope when the bars were about five feet apart. So we were going to move five feet at a time.

There was a short brown rope tied to the bar I was holding. That was my anchor. I tied the free end of that rope to a rock.

Now came the test. I pulled on the main rope. But

nothing happened. I looked around, wondering what I'd done wrong. Then I pulled again, harder. The raft jerked, then started to slide toward me, making a crunching sound on the gravel.

Once the raft got started, I had no trouble keeping it going. I just kept pulling on the rope, hand over hand.

When the two bars were almost touching, I stopped and spent a long time getting the short brown rope untied from the rock. All of the pulling had tightened the knots. I had a knife in my pocket now and could have cut that rope, but it was short enough to begin with, and I needed every inch of it.

When I finally got the knot undone, I knew I had to find a better way. I needed some kind of clip, some way to hook that bar to the rocks without tying a knot. I looked at the straps on the raft, trying to figure out how I could use them. Then I picked up my life jacket, wondering if I could cut off one of the buckles.

I held the jacket in my hand for two or three minutes before the obvious answer came to me. I didn't need to cut off the buckles. I could use the jacket as a big clip.

I tied the bar to the back of the life jacket. Then all I had to do was buckle the jacket around a rock and start hauling on the pulley rope. Once I got my system working, I usually didn't even have to unbuckle the jacket. I lifted it off the old rock and slid it over the next one.

At first everything worked beautifully. I moved the jacket from rock to rock and soon had the raft across the gravel bar and headed uphill. But then things got hard again.

If I'd had a smooth path, my job would have been easy. But I had to haul the raft up over the piles of rocks. The raft kept getting caught, jammed behind a rock. I ended up yanking on the pulley rope, then running over and lifting the raft over a rock, then going back and yanking. When that didn't work, I tried to lift a corner of the raft with one hand while I pulled on the rope with the other. But I was getting nowhere. The ground was just too rough for my system.

I felt like crying. At first everything had looked so good. I had hauled the raft a long way from the water. I had a great system—it just didn't work.

I sat down on a boulder and stared at the hill above me, looking for an easier path. But I knew better. Between me and the top of the hill was a rock pile. No matter how hard I looked, no magic path was going to appear.

It was maddening to have come that far and then be stuck. But all I could see above me was rocks—big ones, sharp ones. Nothing but rocks. No magic path.

The idea came to me all at once. I felt like the guy in the comic strip who has a lightbulb turn on over his head. What made it happen was thinking about the magic path. If I didn't have a magic path, I could build one of my own.

I headed back to the shore and got the limb I'd used to flip the raft. I carried that uphill and set it on the rocks just in front of the raft. Then I went down to the pile of driftwood where I'd gotten that limb.

I found four more limbs in that pile and two more in another pile. I set the limbs a foot or two apart, wherever I could get them to sit on the rocks. They made me think of weird railroad ties.

But I had a path. Once I got the raft up onto the first limb, it slid forward easily on the slick limbs. My magic path soon ran out, though. So I had to keep getting the limbs from the back and moving them ahead of the raft again.

It was slow going. Drive-you-crazy slow. I'd hook the life jacket to a rock, pull the raft forward a few feet, move some limbs, pull the raft forward again. Then change the life jacket and move some more limbs.

And, of course, sometimes the limbs slipped, and the raft got stuck, and the ropes got tangled. And I slipped and fell again and again. My knees were skinned and bleeding, and my hands were banged up. Sweat kept dripping off my forehead and getting into my eyes.

But whenever I looked downhill and saw how far I'd come, I'd start to smile. I was making it. It wasn't easy, and it sure wasn't smooth or pretty. But I was making it.

When I finally stretched out the ropes and buckled the life jacket around that tree, I let out a yell. James looked up at me and waved. Dad was lying at the river's edge, with his hand under the water.

"I got a surprise for you," I yelled.

James jumped up and came running over to the cliff. "What is it?"

"A raft."

CHAPTER ELEVEN

While I was shoving the raft the last few inches, I was surprised to see Dad come out of the sleeping bag. He scooted over to the edge of the river and stuck his whole head under the water. He sat back for a second, then did it again.

"All right, Dad!" I said out loud. If that didn't wake him up, nothing would. And we needed him awake.

Dad said something to James, and James yelled, "Wait! Dad says not to push it over."

"Why not?"

After James listened to Dad for a minute, he called, "Use a rope. Wrap it around the tree two times."

That seemed dumb, but I wasn't going to argue. I unbuckled my life jacket from the tree trunk, cut it free from the metal bar, and tossed it over the cliff. Then I pulled up the safety rope, which was still tied to the trunk. I sawed through the rope just beyond the granny knots, then tied that cut end to a D ring in the front of the raft. After stretching out the rest of the rope, I wrapped it around the trunk of the tree, up above the old knots. To be safe, I decided to make three wraps around the tree.

"Here it comes," I yelled.

I got on my knees and shoved the raft over the edge of the cliff. When I finally had it almost tipping, I braced myself, holding the rope in both hands, and pushed the raft with my feet. The raft slid over the side. The pine tree shook when the rope went tight. I sat there holding on to my end of the rope, but nothing was happening. Dad's idea had worked too well. The raft was hanging in the air, banging against the cliff, about four feet down.

I tried to loosen the rope around the tree, but that didn't work at first. That rope had cut into the bark, and it was holding solid.

I decided that I shouldn't have made three wraps around the trunk. I coiled up the rest of the rope into a loop, then carried it to the tree. I passed the loop around the trunk and yanked the rope free. The two loops that were left began to move.

Once the rope started to slide, I couldn't stop it. For a few seconds, I passed the rope hand over hand, but when I couldn't do it fast enough, I had to let go. I heard the raft hit the ground with a thump.

"Way to go!" James yelled.

I looked over the side and saw the raft. For once I'd been lucky: The thing had landed right side up.

While James was getting the rope loose from the raft, I tied my end to the tree with another six-granny-knot job. Then I looked over the cliff.

"Wait," James called. He ran over to where Dad was sitting. After a minute he yelled, "Dad says you need your gloves." I waited while James ran to the river bag for the gloves. Then he had to put a rock in each one and throw them up to me. "Dad says to walk down the cliff."

I was scared, but there was no use wasting time. I pulled on the gloves and grabbed the rope. I pulled it tight against the trunk and backed over the cliff.

Coming down wasn't as hard as I thought it would be. The cliff had all kinds of cracks and juts. It was almost like climbing down a ladder.

But then I started thinking about how far we had to go before dark. Trying to hurry, I moved my upper foot before the lower one was solid, and they both went sliding down the rock.

I held tight to the rope and ended up hanging there,

swinging back and forth. My shoulder banged against the cliff, and I swung away again.

There was nothing to do but slide down the rope. And that's what I did—faster than I wanted. I was thankful for the gloves.

"Are you okay?" James asked.

"Let's get this thing in the water," I said.

James grabbed the painter and pulled. I shoved on the back. Once we got the raft moving, it slid across the sand.

We took the raft straight to the water. Then, once it was floating, we hauled it upstream to where Dad was sitting. He smiled and raised his fist when we came close.

Dad scooted over to the raft. We helped him to his feet, and he sat down on the edge of the raft. Then he put his head between his knees. "Dizzy," he whispered.

James and I stuffed everything into the river bags. I carried them over and set them in the raft. I tied them down the best I could.

We had lost our paddles, but there were two spares strapped to the raft. James took one and put the other one in the back of the raft. I didn't figure Dad would be using it much.

James and I put on our life jackets. Dad was still sitting on the edge of the raft, his head down. We helped him with his life jacket, and I snapped the buckles. "You ready?" I asked.

He looked up at me and nodded. Then he raised his head slowly and glanced around. "Go up first. Then ferry." He pointed toward the rapids, then turned his hand. "Sideways." Talking seemed to tire him out. When he finished, he held on to the raft and closed his eyes for a minute.

"You need help getting in?" I asked.

Dad shook his head. He leaned back and lifted his legs into the raft one at a time. He sat there for a second, then slid down onto the floor of the raft.

"Hop in," James yelled. "I can handle this."

I climbed in and got my oars ready. I glanced back at Dad. His face was white, but his eyes were open.

James gave the raft a push, then scrambled over the side. "Let's go," he yelled.

I rowed upstream the old-fashioned way, not looking where I was going. Then Dad mumbled something, and I headed for the middle. "Sideways," he said after a minute. I dug in the right oar, hoping that was what he wanted.

The V looked smaller than it did when I was swimming. I had the raft almost broadside when we went over. We hit bottom and shot out to the right. Waves poured over us, but we kept moving. We climbed up one wave, then smacked down hard, with water spraying over us. The next waves were smaller, and in a minute we were just rocking along.

"Nice going," James yelled.

"It's easier in a raft," I shouted.

James was looking toward the shore. "You took the raft up that?" he asked.

I looked back at the rocky slope. "It didn't fly up there," I said.

Dad leaned forward. "Amazing," he said.

"What?"

"You," he said. "Amazing."

I looked back at him. He had unwrapped his hand and was dipping the shirt in the water. The hand looked awful.

"We're gonna make it," I yelled.

"Piece of cake," James said.

"Yeah," Dad said quietly. "Piece of cake."

CHAPTER TWELVE

We drifted along for a while. I only used the oars to keep the raft in the middle of the current.

Dad reached out and tapped me on the back. "Water," he whispered.

James handed me a water bottle, and I reached back and held it up to Dad's mouth. I got some water into his mouth, but most of it dribbled down his chin. He pushed the bottle away.

Then his whole body jerked, and he vomited. "Get me something to clean this up," I yelled to James. I used my hand to brush the vomit away from Dad's chin. James handed me a wet sweatshirt, and I wiped off Dad's mouth and neck. I tried to clean up the life jacket, but it still smelled awful.

"It's okay," Dad said. His eyes were only halfway open.

"We're coming to something," James yelled.

Dad didn't seem to hear him.

"Dad!" I yelled. "What do I do?"

Dad's eyes snapped open. He leaned to the side and looked past me. "Straight," he said, then flopped back and closed his eyes.

I guided the raft into the V, and we shot through a stretch of rough water. James had a system where he did three quick strokes on one side, then switched to the other for three. It seemed to work.

When the river flattened out enough so that I could look back at Dad, his eyes were closed, and spit was dribbling from the side of his mouth.

I reached back and grabbed his leg. "Dad! You've gotta stay awake." His eyes opened a crack. "Come on! You can't sleep now!"

"Pour water on me," he said.

"What?"

"I mean it."

"James," I said, "hand me the milk jug."

James unclipped the milk jug and gave it to me. I reached over the side and scooped up some water.

For a second I held the jug above Dad's head. Then I dumped it.

Dad's whole body jerked, and he let out a big "Oooo." But his eyes came open.

"I'm sorry," I told him. "But you've gotta help me."

"Water," he said.

I held his chin with one hand and the water bottle with the other. I poured a few drops into his mouth, then a few more. He had trouble swallowing, and some of the water came back up. But I was pretty sure he'd gotten a little.

I clipped the milk jug to a D ring by my foot. I might have to wake him up in a hurry.

"I think I hear something," James said.

I looked back at Dad. "What do we do?"

Dad leaned to the side, then looked up at the hills on the right. "I don't know."

"Come on, Dad." I grabbed the wet sweatshirt I'd used earlier, reached out, and dipped it in the water. Then I leaned back and wiped Dad's face.

He pushed the sweatshirt away. "Dizzy, I don't know where we are." He looked up at me. "Better stop."

I don't know if I would have stopped or not. But by then it was too late. The current was picking up, and the roar ahead of us was getting loud. I kept the raft in the middle of the stream and hoped for the best.

"Take a look," I yelled over my shoulder. "Tell me what to do."

If Dad said anything, I didn't hear him. The river was getting choppy, and I was rowing slowly, trying to keep us straight and steady.

"It's a drop!" James yelled.

Before we hit the V, I could see the water below us. So the drop was pretty small. We'd been through worse.

When the raft dipped down, I wasn't even worried. It wasn't a drop-off, just a little slide into a pool. I raised the oars out of the water, ready to row us forward when we hit.

The raft smacked the surface of the pool, and we shot forward.

Then, just as I was starting to row, the raft stopped cold. I slid forward in the seat.

I didn't understand it. We were supposed to be flying through the rough water, and we weren't moving at all.

Then I felt the back of the raft dip down, and I suddenly realized what was happening. The current had the front of the raft pinned against a rock. And, like water pouring over a dam, the same current was sending a wave of water spilling into our raft.

Then Dad rose up from the floor of the raft and came diving over me. His knee hit the side of my head, and he smacked down close to James.

The sudden shift of weight caused the raft to rock, and the current sent us spinning. A wave crashed against us, soaking me with icy water. But we were moving forward again.

Even then, while I was fighting the waves, I knew I'd just seen something that would stay with me all my life. Dad had come awake with the water pouring over him and had immediately gone into action. While I was still figuring out the problem, he had saved us.

When we hit calmer water, James yelled, "Give me the milk jug. I got a lot of bailing to do."

Dad lay on the floor of the raft, with the water sloshing around him. His knees were pulled up to his chest, and his whole body was shaking. James worked around him, dumping jug after jug of water over the side.

I rowed slowly, keeping us in the current. When James had gotten rid of most of the water, I guided the raft to the bank and hauled in the oars. "Let's help Dad into the back again," I said.

James got down by Dad's head. "Dad," he said. "Daddy." Then James looked up at me with tears in his eyes. "Help him!" I moved up beside James and looked into Dad's face.

I hope I never see another face like that in my life.

It was twisted out of shape with pain. It didn't look like Dad's face. It didn't even look human. He had bitten through his lower lip, and blood was running down his chin. Groaning sobs were coming out of his mouth.

"What'll we do?" James asked.

"There's nothing to do," I said. "He's passed out."

"He landed right on his hurt arm."

"He saved us," I said. "If he hadn't made that dive, we'd have gone under back there."

"I know it," James said. "But he—" He stopped and shook his head.

I thought about letting Dad stay where he was, but the raft was off balance. We eased him over onto his back, with his bad hand across his chest. Then we slid him over the rower's bench. We tried to be careful, but he was heavy and hard to move. He got banged and bounced all the way. He groaned some, but he seemed to be unconscious. I hoped he was.

We got Dad stretched out, with his head against the back of the raft. Then we moved back to our places. James took a long drink from the water bottle and passed it to me. "What do we do now?"

"Keep going, I guess." I put in the oars and ferried us back into the current.

James nodded, but didn't say anything.

We floated along for a while. I was too tired to think ahead. I just kept the raft steady.

"You hear the noise?" James called.

Once he said that, I noticed the growling sound too. I looked back at Dad. He hadn't moved at all. His face was still twisted, and his body twitched now and then. But he seemed to be out cold.

I thought about chancing a run, just heading into the rough water and making the best of it. But I knew better. Dad had said it this morning: The fastest way was to do things right the first time.

I steered the raft toward the bank. James looked back at me. "Come on," he said. "We can't quit now."

"We're not quitting," I said. "But I have to check it out before we run it."

We moved up close to shore, and James jumped out with the painter in his hand. He held the raft while I ran ahead and looked at the rapids.

From then on, that's what we did. I didn't always know what I was looking for, but by checking the rapids first, I could plan which way to go. Once in a while, we ended going somewhere I didn't plan to, but we fought our way through.

Hours went by, and the sun got lower in the sky. I rowed most of the time, trying to hurry us along. And James paddled.

For a while my back and arms hurt so much that I

thought I'd have to stop. But I'd rest a few minutes, then go back to rowing. My hands blistered, and then the blisters broke. Once I tried to take off the gloves, but by then they were stuck to my hands.

I just kept rowing. Sometimes I was almost asleep. I'd give a jump and realize that I couldn't remember the last few minutes. But my arms kept moving.

Just before sundown James yelled, "Look." He was pointing his paddle toward the hillside on our left.

I looked up and saw a brown bear standing in an open spot. He was watching us, but he didn't look interested.

I wasn't too interested either. I watched him for a minute, then turned back to the river. And I kept rowing.

"We're gonna make it," I said to James.

James looked back and smiled. "Piece of cake."

CHAPTER THIRTEEN

It was almost dark when we spotted the lights of Walling's Landing up ahead of us. The sun had gone down a while before, and the air was getting chilly.

"There it is!" James yelled.

I looked back at Dad. He was still on the floor of the raft. Once, an hour or two before, he had let out a moan, but that was all. "We're home," I said to him, knowing he couldn't hear me.

The last quarter mile took forever. The current was gone, and I had to row us in. All of a sudden my chewed-up hands were on fire, and my arms were cramping.

It was all I could do to keep the oars moving.

When we got close enough so that we could see somebody on the docks, I started to yell: "Call 911! We need a helicopter! Snakebite!"

By the time I yelled that twice, a deep voice answered back. "Okay, son. We hear you."

Then I heard an outboard motor, and a boat came roaring up to meet us. A man in overalls yelled, "Throw me your line." He held on to our painter and towed us to the dock.

Everything was crazy after that. People were all around us, yelling and running back and forth. James and I stood back while Lucky and some of the rafting guides worked on Dad.

A woman handed me a bottle of lemonade, and I drank the whole thing at once. A little later she came over, took the empty bottle, and handed me another one. I sat down on the dock and then couldn't keep my head up. I turned sideways and lay down.

Lying there, I couldn't see what they were doing to Dad's arm. I didn't want to look anyway.

After a while they carried Dad away in a stretcher. "Stay here, son," Lucky said to me. "I'll be right back."

"These boys aren't going anywhere," a woman said. She was sitting with her arm around James.

A few minutes later Lucky was kneeling beside me. "They're taking your dad over to the helicopter pad," he said. "The chopper should be here pretty soon. I wish you boys could go out with them, but there's no room."

"That's okay," I said.

"I called your mother," Lucky went on.

I started to tell him that she was James's mother, not mine. But it was just too much trouble.

"She's on her way to the hospital. She may beat the helicopter. I told her you'd stay here tonight. I'll take you down there in the morning."

"Can't we go now?" James asked.

"I think you boys better get some rest," Lucky said. "You've had a rough time."

"You know what my big brother did?" James said. "He hauled the raft clear up a mountain."

Somebody fixed some soup for us, but I couldn't handle a spoon with my gloves on, and my hands were shaking too much anyway.

"Let me feed you," the woman said. She gave me a few spoonfuls before I waved her away.

My head was just too heavy. I pushed my bowl aside and leaned forward onto the table.

The next thing I knew James was pulling on my shoulder. "Greg, you gotta wake up."

I was in a sleeping bag in a tent. I couldn't figure out what was happening. "How'd I get here?" I asked.

James laughed. "Lucky carried you. You went to sleep at the table, and you didn't wake up at all. Not even when they bandaged up your hands. They had to cut off your gloves with scissors."

I looked at the gauze pads on my hands. "What time is it?"

"Eight o'clock. Come on. We gotta eat. Then Lucky's gonna take us to see Dad. Mom called this morning, and she said Dad's gonna be okay."

Before breakfast I called my mother in San Francisco and told her what had happened. I made things sound better than they were, but she still wanted to drive up and get me. I talked her out of that, but I had to promise to have a doctor check me over and to call her again afterward.

When we drove off in Lucky's pickup, we passed the pink bus. I realized that it was only yesterday morning that we had ridden on that bus. It seemed like a year ago.

Driving along the twisting roads Lucky played heavy metal music on his tape player. James sat close to me and jabbered a lot: "Have you ever been in a hospital? I haven't. Not since I was born anyway. I know a lot about hospitals, though. I had this baby-sitter who used to watch *General Hospital* every day."

"Dad's gonna be fine," I said.

When we got to the hospital, Dad was awake—barely. He gave us a tired smile, but he didn't try to talk.

James's mother hugged James and cried and fussed over his blistered hands.

"I'm fine," James said. "I'm fine."

"You are not," she said. "Those hands are awful. I'm going to get a doctor to look at them."

I put my beat-up hands behind my back. Dad saw me do it and winked.

Right then I figured he was going to be all right.

And he was, more or less. His hand was always a little stiff after that, but he said he was thankful the doctors had saved it. He said he'd reached up and put his hand right on the rattlesnake, which must have been asleep on the boulder. I still get chills thinking about that.

James and I got our pictures in the newspaper, and we were on the local TV news. We were at the hospital when the program came on, but James's mother had set up her VCR to record it.

Later that night James and I watched the program and kept reversing the tape and seeing our part over and over. The woman on the news called us *brave young heroes.*

"You think we're brave young heroes?" James asked me.

I just laughed.

"You're a hero," James said. "But what about me? What if they found out I was crying? I was so scared, I almost wet my pants."

"So what?" I said. "I was scared too. How could we not be scared?"

"But we won't tell, will we?" James said. "That's nobody's business, right?'

"Right," I said. "We got down the river, and Dad's going to be okay. That's all that matters."

"I'm gonna take this tape to school," James said. "I'm gonna show it to my class."

In a way I wished that I could take the tape to my school. Except for a few of my friends, nobody in San Francisco ever heard about my trip. And not even my friends knew how rough it had been.

It seemed funny to me, like I had a secret nobody knew. I felt cheated. After what I had been through, things shouldn't have been the same. But they were.

Except with Dad. We got along better after that. When I saw him each month, he usually had me plan our day. We talked more than we did before. And the quiet times were easier. He didn't try to keep things going with a bunch of questions.

James came with Dad whenever he could. And, like always, he did plenty of talking. He loved to tell people about how he and his big brother had saved his dad's life. But the way he told it, nobody took him seriously.

So I'd had an adventure, and nothing was any different. At least that's what I thought at first.

But then came that Saturday in October. James and I were in my kitchen in San Francisco. We had spent the day hiking at Point Reyes, and Dad had dropped us off while he did some shopping.

We were drinking orange juice, and James was rattling on about a splatterball game. I didn't understand splatterball, but it didn't matter. He was doing all the talking.

Then there was a crash. It felt like something hitting the building. "What—?" James started.

I knew what it was. I slid under the kitchen table and pulled James down with me. "It's an earthquake," I said.

By then, he had figured it out. The floor was shaking, and cupboard doors were flying open. Soup cans hit the floor and rolled. The refrigerator came sliding away from the wall.

"We gotta move this thing," I said. Staying underneath, James and I scooted the table across the floor until we were halfway through the wide doorway into the living room. "Perfect," I yelled. I heard glass breaking somewhere. And a dog was howling.

Crouching there under the table, I remembered back to that other time when James and I were sitting helpless on the riverbank while Dad lay with his hand in the water. Nothing—not even an earthquake—could be worse than that.

And that's when I realized that something *had* changed. Me. I'm not saying that I wasn't scared. If you're not scared during an earthquake, there's something wrong with you. But I wasn't going to panic. Whatever came next, I was ready.

"We're okay," I told James.

"What'll we do?" James yelled.

"Wait till it stops."

A jar of applesauce hit the floor and shattered, sending pieces of glass flying around us.

"Then what?" James asked.

"We'll figure that out when it stops."

James looked over at me and smiled. "Piece of cake," he said.